Christmas 2003

To Ryan
   With love from
      Grandma & Grandpa Scott

My Little Prayers

**Illustrations by
Stephanie McFetridge Britt**

Compiled by Brenda Ward

Tommy
NELSON®

www.tommynelson.com

A Division of Thomas Nelson, Inc.
www.ThomasNelson.com

My Little Prayers
Copyright © 1993 by Word Publishing. Illustrations © 1993 by
Stephanie McFetridge Britt. All rights reserved. No portion of this
book may be reproduced in any form, except for brief quotations
in reviews, without written permission from the publisher.

Published in Nashville, Tennessee, by Tommy Nelson®, a Division
of Thomas Nelson, Inc.

The publisher has made every effort to locate the owners of all
copyrighted material and to obtain permission to reprint the
prayers in this book. Any errors are unintentional, and
corrections will be made in future editions if necessary. The
publishers acknowledge special thanks for permission received
from the following:

Celebration for "The Butterfly Song" by Brian Howard, copyright ©
1974, 1975 by Celebration. "A Great Gray Elephant" courtesy of the
National Society to Prevent Blindness. "Sometimes by Step" by
Rich Mullins, copyright © 1992 BMG Songs, Inc./Kid Brothers of
St. Frank Publishing.

Scripture quotations identified ICB are from *The International Children's
Bible®, New Century Version®*, copyright © 1983, 1986, 1988, by Word
Publishing, Dallas, TX. Used by permission.
Entries marked KJV are from the King James Version.

Library of Congress Cataloging–in–Publication Data:

My little prayers / illustrations by Stephanie McFetridge Britt:
    compiled by Brenda C. Ward
        p. cm.
        Summary: A collection of simple prayers arranged in
    such categories as "My Mealtime," My Feelings," "My
    Special Days," and "My Bedtime."
        ISBN 0-8499-1064-1
        1. Children—Prayer-books and devotions—English.
    [1. Prayers.] I. Britt, Stephanie, ill. II. Ward, Brenda C.
    BV265.M896 1993
        242'.62—dc20
                                                    93-578
                                                    CIP
                                                    AC

Printed in the United States of America
03 04 05 06 07 LBM 25 24 23 22 21

CONTENTS

**The Lord is all I need.
He takes care of me.**

PSALM 16:5

MY DAY

Day by day, dear Lord, of Thee
Three things I pray:
To see Thee more clearly,
Love Thee more dearly,
Follow Thee more nearly,
Day by day.

St. Richard of Chichester

10

Oh God, You are my God,
  And I will ever praise You.
I will seek You in the morning,
And I will learn to walk in Your
  ways.
And step by step You'll lead me,
And I will follow You all of my
  days.

Rich Mullins

For this new morning with its
    light,
For rest and shelter of the night,
For health and food,
For love and friends,
For every gift Your goodness
    sends,
We thank You, gracious Lord.
    Amen.

Traditional

All for You, dear God.
  Everything I do,
Or think,
Or say,
The whole day long.
Help me to be good.

Unknown

When the weather is wet,
 We must not fret.
When the weather is cold,
 We must not scold.
When the weather is warm,
 We must not storm . . .
Be thankful together,
 Whatever the weather.

Unknown

He gives food to every living creature. His love continues forever.

Psalm 136:25

MY MEALTIME

God is great.
    God is good.
    Let us thank Him
    for our food.

Traditional

Thank you for the world so sweet,
   Thank you for the food we eat,
Thank you for the birds that sing,
Thank you, God, for everything!

E. Rutter Leatham

The Lord is good to me,
    and so I thank the Lord.
For giving me the things I need:
    the sun, the rain, and the
    apple seed!
The Lord is good to me.

Traditional

God, we thank you for this food,
   For rest and home and all
      things good;
For wind and rain and sun above,
But most of all for those we love.

Maryleona Frost

**I go to bed and sleep in peace.
Lord, only you keep me safe.**

<small>PSALM 4:8</small>

MY BEDTiMe

Now I lay me down to sleep.
I pray Thee, Lord, my soul to
keep.
Your love be with me through
the night
And wake me with the morning
light.

Traditional

Lord, keep us safe this night,
Secure from all our fears.
May angels guard us while we
   sleep,
Till morning light appears.

Traditional

Lord, with Your praise we drop off to sleep.
Carry us through the night,
Make us fresh for the morning.
Hallelujah for the day!
And blessing for the night!

from a Ghanaian fisherman's prayer

Father, we thank You for the
    night,
And for the pleasant morning
    light,
For rest and food and loving
    care,
And all that makes the day so
    fair.

Help us to do the things we
    should,
To be to others kind and good;
In all we do and all we say,
To grow more loving every day.

Unknown

Children, obey your parents the way the Lord wants. This is the right thing to do.

Ephesians 6:1

MY FAMILY AND FRIENDS

God bless all those that I love.
  God bless all those that
     love me.
God bless all those that love
those that I love, and all those
that love those who love me.

New England Sampler

Thank You for my parents, Lord,
  and all the fun we've had.
There's no time I love better
  than with my mom and dad.

Help me, Lord, to always know
  the many ways they care.
For toys and snacks and big
  bear hugs
  and always being there,

When I grow up, I want to be
  just like my parents, too.
Because they make me feel
  so great
  and love me just like You.

Beth Burt

May the road rise to meet you,
May the wind be always at
your back,
May the sun shine warm on
your face,
The rain fall softly on your
fields;
And until we meet again,
May God hold you in the palm
of His hand.

Traditional, Irish

Dear Lord,
Thank You for my grandparents.
They always have time to read
   to me or play games.
They like to tickle and play
   and laugh.
And they like ice cream and
   going to the park, too.
Mostly though, God, they love
   me.
Please take care of them, Lord.
I think they must be a lot like
   You.

Anonymous

Our family's big, our house is
    small;
We're crowded as can be.
But, Father, there's a lot of love
That's shared here happily.

I love my mom and daddy, too;
They keep me safe each day.
But thanks for brothers and
    sisters, Lord;
They have more time to play.

Mary Hollingsworth

**The Lord is my shepherd.
I have everything I need.**

PSALM 23:1

MY FAVORITE THINGS

Please give me what I ask,
      dear Lord,
If You'd be glad about it.
But if You think it's not for me,
Please help me do without it.

Traditional

Dear Father,
    Hear and bless
        Thy beasts and singing
            birds.
    And guard with tenderness
        Small things that have no
            words.

Unknown

A great gray elephant,
  A little yellow bee,
A tiny purple violet,
  A tall green tree,
A red and white sailboat
  On a blue sea—
All these things
  You gave to me,
When you made
  My eyes to see—
Thank you, God.

*National Society
for the Prevention
of Blindness, Inc.*

If I were a butterfly,
I'd thank You, Lord, for giving
me wings,
And if I were a robin in a tree,
I'd thank You, Lord, that I could
sing,
And if I were a fish in the sea,
I'd wiggle my tail, and I'd giggle
with glee,
But I just thank You, Father,
for making me *me*.

Brian Howard

**When I am afraid,
I will trust you.**

Psalm 56:3

MY FEELINGS

Dear Lord,
  Thank You that I am sometimes
    strong,
    help me when I am still weak;
Thank You that I am sometimes
    wise,
    help me when I am still
    foolish;
Thank You that sometimes I
    have done well,
    forgive me the times I have
    failed You;
And teach me to serve You and
    Your world
    with love and faith and truth,
    with hope and grace and good
    humor. Amen

A Swaledale Parish Prayer

64

I feel happy, Jesus!
I am happy when I laugh with
   friends, or hold a puppy.
I feel happy eating ice cream, or
   listening to a story.
I feel happy when someone
   says, "I love you."
Lord, I am happy because I
   belong to You!
That is the best thing of all to be
   happy about!

Sheryl Crawford

Dear God, my friend is moving,
   and I'm so sad.
We've had so much fun together,
   and I don't want her to move.
Please help her to find new
   friends where she's going so
   she won't be lonely.
And help me to make new
   friends, too.
Thank You, Jesus, for being my
   best friend.

Anonymous

68

Dear God, be good to me.
The sea is so wide,
and my boat is so small.

The Breton Fisherman's Prayer

Jesus, someone I care for lives
    with You now.
I feel very sad because that person
    is not here.
Sometimes I cry . . . to let the
    sadness out.
Lord, You say that people who
    live with You are happy.
In heaven, there are angels and
    friends and family.
Jesus, please help me to remember
    that someday we will be together
    again with the ones we love . . .
And we will live forever with
    You in heaven!

Sheryl Crawford

**This is the day that the Lord has made.
Let us rejoice and be glad today!**

PSALM 118:24

MY
SPECIAL
DAYS

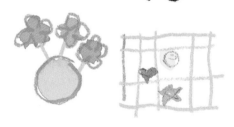

MY BIRTHDAY

Dear Lord, I am happy today
  because it is MY BIRTHDAY!
I was born on a day like today.
It was a great day for my family,
  one they could never forget.
Thank You for fun things,
  like cake and candles,
  for family and friends and
  presents and birthday cards.
But most of all Lord, thank You
  for giving me life!

Sheryl Crawford

CHRISTMAS

What can I give Him,
  Poor as I am?
If I were a shepherd,
  I would bring Him a lamb.
If I were a wise man,
  I would do my part.
But what can I give Him?
  Give Him my heart.

Christina G. Rossetti

CHRISTMAS

Away in a manger, no crib for a
   bed,
The little Lord Jesus laid down
   His sweet head;
The stars in the sky looked
   down where He lay,
The little Lord Jesus, asleep on
   the hay.

Be near me, Lord Jesus; I ask
   Thee to stay
Close by me for ever, and love
   me, I pray;
Bless all the dear children in
   Thy tender care,
Prepare us for heaven, to live
   with Thee there.

Martin Luther

EASTER

He is Lord,
  He is Lord!
He is risen from the dead
  and He is Lord!
Every knee shall bow;
Every tongue confess,
  that Jesus Christ is Lord.

Traditional

The Lord listens when I pray to him.
PSALM 4:3

MY
TIME
WITH GOD

Two little eyes to look to God;
Two little ears to hear His word;
Two little feet to walk in His
    ways;
Two little lips to sing His praise;
Two little hands to do His will;
And one little heart to love Him
    still.

Traditional

All things bright and beautiful,
All creatures great and small,
All things wise and wonderful,
The Lord God made them all.

He gave us eyes to see them,
And lips that we might tell
How great is God Almighty,
Who has made all things well!

Carl Frances Alexander

God be in my head
  And in my understanding.
God be in mine eyes
And in my looking.
God be in my mouth
And in my speaking.
God be in my heart
And in my thinking.

Unknown

THE LORD'S PRAYER

Our Father which art in heaven
   Hallowed be thy name.
Thy kingdom come.
Thy will be done
   in earth, as it is in heaven.
Give us this day our daily bread.
And forgive us our trespasses,
As we forgive those who trespass
   against us.
And lead us not into temptation,
But deliver us from evil:
For thine is the kingdom,
And the power, and the glory,
For ever. Amen.

Matthew 6:9–13 KJV

92